# Fancy Nancy

## and the Sensational Babysitter

Based on *Fancy Nancy* written by Jane O'Connor

Cover illustration by Robin Preiss Glasser

Interior illustrations by Aleksey and Olga Ivanov

HARPER FESTIVAL

*An Imprint of HarperCollinsPublishers*

HarperFestival is an imprint of HarperCollins Publishers.

Fancy Nancy and the Sensational Babysitter
Text copyright © 2010 by Jane O'Connor
Illustrations copyright © 2010 by Robin Preiss Glasser
www.harpercollinschildrens.com
Library of Congress catalog card number: 2009939631
ISBN 978-0-06-170378-2

Book design by Sean Boggs
13 14 15 16 17 CWM 20 19 18 17 16 15 14 13 12 11
❖
First Edition

Tonight our parents are going to the movies.
A new babysitter is coming.
Her name is Alex and she is a teenager.
I am very excited.

I help my sister get into her pj's.
I hope she goes to sleep early.
Then Alex and I will have lots of time together.

I make an agenda for the evening's activities.
An agenda is like a list, only fancier.
This evening will be so enjoyable—that's fancy for fun.

First we'll play with my dolls.
Then we can play dress up.
Or maybe Alex will bring some fashion magazines.
We can look through them and pick our favorite ensembles.
(That's a fancy word for outfits.)

Soon I hear my mom calling,
"Come meet Alex."
I run downstairs.

I am very confused. In fact, I am stupefied.
A teenager is in our living room—a boy teenager.
"Where is Alex?" I ask.
"I'm Alex," he says.

Oh no!
This is practically a babysitting tragedy.
But I try to be polite.
I hold out my hand and say, "*Enchanté.*"
(That's French for "pleased to meet you.")

My sister and Alex are building with her blocks.
Alex asks me to come play with them.

Instead, I go upstairs to my room.

Alex can't help being a boy.

Still, seeing my agenda makes me a little melancholy,

which is fancy for sad.

I am reading a book to my doll Marabelle
when there is a knock on the door.
"Entrez," I say. (That's French for "come in.")
It is Alex.
"Your sister is asleep," he says.

"Wow! You got her to bed so early.
And she didn't even cry."
He asks if I want to learn to juggle.
"Oui, oui, oui," I say.

We go downstairs.
Alex finds four tennis balls.

Ooh la la!
Alex is an expert at juggling.
He can keep four balls in the air.

I try to juggle three—impossible!
Even two is very hard.
(If you don't believe me, try it yourself.)

Then I show Alex my hula hoop.
"Wow! I always wanted to learn to do that,"
he says.

"I can teach you," I say.
I demonstrate how to hula.
(Demonstrate is a fancy word for show.)
Not to brag, but I can hula
hoop for soooo long.

Alex tries to hula.
He looks so funny!
Still, I try hard not to giggle because
that would be very rude.

Whew! We are both thirsty now.
We need refreshments.

I put cookies on a plate.
We drink lemonade out of teacups.
I remind Alex to keep his pinky up.
It is fancier that way.

When my parents come home
I tell them, "Alex is a sensational babysitter.
I hope he comes again soon."

Alex turns and bows. "Merci, Nancy!"